TED 1

Hi my name is Tractor Ted.
This is my book all about tractors.

TED 1

Here is a big tractor.
The farmer sits in the cab.

Inside is the steering wheel and all the controls.

TED 1

The tractor has big tyres to help it across the fields.

On the back is a hitch.

TED 1

The farmer can use the hitch to pull a trailer,

a plough to plough the fields,

TED 1

or a seed drill to plant the seed.

The tractor can pull a mower,

TED 1

a baler to bale up the hay,

or a straw chopper
to make a cosy bed.

TED 1

On the front of the tractor the farmer can use a spike to lift the straw from the trailer,

a bucket to move the grain,

or a bale handler.

It can carry a wrapped bale
without making holes in it.

TED 1

The tractor can even carry heavy bags,

or use a buckrake to push up
a big pile of grass silage.

TED 1

Tractors come in different colours.
There are blue ones,

red ones,

TED 1

green ones and

yellow ones.

TED 1

Tractors can drive along roads,

or across fields.

TED 1

Tractors can be small,

or really big.

TED 1

Some do not have tyres they have caterpillar tracks.

They will help the tractor drive across very muddy fields without getting stuck.

TED 1

How many tyres can you count on this tractor?

What colour are these tractors?

What has the farmer hitched on?

TED 1